Will she die?

Colin Terrell
Michael Terrell

First published in Great Britain by Axis Education Ltd.

ISBN 978-1-84618-196-2

Axis Education, PO Box 459
Shrewsbury, SY4 4WZ

Email: enquiries@axiseducation.co.uk
www.axiseducation.co.uk

The prisoner was handcuffed to the table.

'Where is she? Where is she?' yelled DC Ken Green.

The prisoner didn't answer.

Leaning across the table, Green smashed his fist into the prisoner's jaw.

The prisoner slumped sideways, still handcuffed to the table.

Green lifted up his fist to hit him again. 'If that girl dies, nothing will stop me killing you.'

Will she die?

Another policeman grabbed Green's arm. Pointing at the CCTV camera on the wall he said, 'Hit him again and we'll both be in the shit.'

Green glared at the prisoner and snarled, 'Okay, okay. If I stay here I'll kill the bastard.'

He walked to the door. 'I'll go up to the control room. See if there's any news on the girl.'

★★★★

Outside the door stood Green's boss, DI Dave Martin. The only black DI in the area.

He'd been watching what was happening on a screen. The DI stood in front of Green. 'Hold on, Green,' he said. 'We've got to be careful.'

He gripped Green by the arms and said, 'We'll wipe out the recording where you just hit him, but there's no way we're going to get the girl if you kill the bastard.'

Letting go of Green's arms the DI said firmly, 'Believe me, I know how you feel. We all feel the same. But we don't know if the girl's even alive.'

'Maybe he's just bullshitting us. Have we got any proof she's still alive, other than his word for it?'

Nodding towards the interview room door Green said, 'The bastard followed the girl's mother into a park. The girl's only five. He hit the mother from behind. When she went down, he grabbed the kid.'

Green's fists were clenched as he went on. 'He was careful to hit the mother when they were close to the park gates. He'd left a car just outside the gates. Witnesses said the girl was screaming and struggling as she was dragged away from her mother. He was wearing a bloody awful looking mask. She was terrified.'

Green put both hands against the wall and looked down at his feet. He took a few deep breaths.

'But he made one mistake. The girl was grabbing at anything. Trying to stop herself from being pushed into the car. Luckily for us she pulled off his mask. We got his face on a CCTV camera outside the park. We got the mask too.'

'So how did you track him down?' asked DI Martin.

'Two of our guys knew him. His name's Carl Dobson. From then on it was dead easy for us. We pulled his address from records. There was lots of stuff on him. GBH.

Burglary. A whole load of crap. Within minutes we were outside his flat waiting. And uniformed officers were at the girl's house.'

Green took another deep breath. 'About four hours after the kidnap the parents had a phone call. Dobson said he wanted a million for the girl. We'd tapped into the phone line.'

He pointed to the interview room door.

'Dobson says he's locked the girl in a box. And unless he gets the money, she'll die. From lack of food. Lack of water. Or just plain fright. Whatever, it'll be a bloody awful way to die.'

The DI nodded his head and Green went on with the story.

'He must have taken the kid somewhere while we were watching his flat. We've no idea where. He'd made a tape and played it over the phone to the parents. They said they could hear their kid screaming. Recognised her voice.'

Green's face started to redden with anger again. 'Then, they heard a thud. Which they said sounded like a box being shut. After that the screams were muffled.'

The DI was shaking his head.

'As far as we can tell, it does sound like the sick bastard may well have locked the kid in some kind of box.'

Green looked at the DI. 'That's all we've got so far,' he said. 'Unless Dobson tells us where the kid is, she's in serious danger. But he is offering us a deal. He's not got much to lose. He knows that whatever happens, it's a long jail term for him – for kidnapping or for murder. He says the deal is that if he tells us where the girl is, we let him off scot-free.'

The DI shook his head and muttered, 'That's some deal.'

Green looked at his boss. 'Just leave me alone with him for ten minutes. He'll tell us where the girl is. Trust me. I'll get him to talk.'

The DI frowned and said, 'You know we can't let that happen. No matter what he's done. We can't just beat it out of him. Even if he is a low-life, Dobson has rights.'

Green glared at Martin, 'Rights!' he yelled. 'What bloody rights? The kid's the only one who should have rights. She's got the right to live. He's got no rights. Not now. Not after what he's done.'

The DI tried to assure his officer, 'Green, let me talk to him. Let's see if I can do something.'

He put his hand on Green's shoulder and said, 'You go back up to the control room and calm down. Find out what's happening before you do something really stupid.'

Green looked at the DI and shouted, 'Come on sir! Just let me back in there. Ten minutes, that's all I need. I'll get it out of him.'

The DI gripped Green by the arm again and said firmly, 'DC Green. This is an order. Go back up to the control room.'

When Green hesitated the DI boomed, 'Now! You either calm down or I'll take you off the case completely. Don't think I'm joking. Keep yelling that you're going to beat him to a pulp and I'll have you arrested.'

DI Martin looked hard at Green, 'I mean it. Don't push me.'

Green glared at his boss for a few seconds. He turned on his heel and marched off down the corridor.

The DI made a quick call upstairs. He asked to see the mask Dobson had been wearing.

When it arrived he sat on a bench. Looking at the mask. Thinking.

****

Will she die?

In the control room Green sat down next to a policewoman. She was wearing earphones. Keeping up with what was happening in the parent's house.

Green tapped her on the shoulder. The PC lifted one of the earphones off to hear him.

'Anything happening?' he asked.

She shook her head. 'There's been plenty of crying. The GP is with the mother now giving her something to calm her down. But there's not a lot happening that's of use to us.'

'How's it going with Dobson?' she asked.

'We're gettin' nowhere. And what's worse,

DI Martin's on duty. All he keeps on about is Dobson's rights.'

Green shook his head, 'Terrorist's rights. Black's rights. Gay's rights. Everybody's fucking rights. Except the girl's.'

Then he added bitterly, 'She's going to die in that box. Simply because she's white and has rich parents. A rich white girl. So she's got no rights. And all Martin's worried about is Dobson's rights.'

There was silence for a few seconds. Green shook his head again and said, 'And guess what? DI Martin was going to arrest me for smacking Dobson.'

The policewoman raised her eyes to the ceiling. 'That's the world now,' she said turning back to her screen. 'All the criminals have rights. No matter what they do.'

★★★★

Meanwhile downstairs DI Martin had been thinking for long enough. He barged through the interview room door and told the police sergeant to leave him alone with Dobson.

Martin sat down opposite Dobson. For a while he looked at the prisoner in silence. Blood still dripped down Dobson's chin.

'Okay,' said DI Martin softly, 'you've got us between a rock and a hard place.' The DI hesitated. 'Let me get this straight. You're saying that if we don't make a deal the girl dies. Is that it?'

A slight smile crept onto Dobson's face. 'That's it,' he said. 'I get a deal. Or she dies.'

Will she die?

The DI nodded and said, 'I've talked with my bosses. Like you'd expect, they ain't happy with this. They don't want a deal.'

Martin hesitated again, 'But this is good news for you because they've left it to me.'

Dobson smiled through blood and broken teeth.

'And about time,' he snarled. 'The girl's not got long.'

Dobson kept talking. Sounding more confident. 'And if you don't do a deal. What do you think the papers and TV will say? They'd say the police killed the girl. Remember. She'll be dead in a couple of days. An' everybody'll think you lot were the real killers.'

DI Martin stayed silent. Thinking.

Finally he said, 'Okay, Dobson. You win. Seems we've got no choice. Tell us where the girl is and you go free.'

Dobson smiled. 'You think I'm stupid or something? Before I tell you anything I want it recorded so I can use it when my case comes up.'

The DI pointed to a CCTV camera on the wall behind Dobson's head.

'See the camera?' the DI asked. 'If the red

light is flashing, everything is being recorded
– pictures and sound.'

Dobson turned and looked at the camera.
He thought for a minute and nodded.

'Okay,' he said. 'This is the deal. I'll tell you
where the girl is. Then you drop the charges.'

The DI quietly muttered, 'Yes'.

'Louder,' scowled Dobson. 'I need this to be
loud and clear on the CCTV tape.'

Raising his voice DI Martin said, 'Okay
Dobson. For the record. Here's the deal. If
you tell us where the girl is, we'll drop all
charges.'

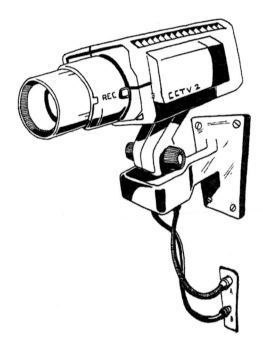

Martin looked at Dobson in disgust. The DI was beginning to lose his rag. 'But you need to tell us right now. No more demands. No more conditions. Where is she?'

Dobson looked at the detective and thought for a moment. Smiling, he said, 'She's in a garage on the West Hill Estate. Number eight.'

Without another word DI Martin leapt up and flew out of the interview room. Turning into the corridor he almost charged into DC Green.

'Green – she's in a garage on the West Hill Estate. Number eight.

Get going,' rattled the DI. 'Let me know on the radio the minute you've got her.'

Green span around and ran back down the corridor.

The DI went back into the interview room. He sat down at the table and looked at Dobson who was drumming his fingers on the table.

After a short silence the DI put his two-way radio on the table and said, 'Now we wait. When I hear the kid's okay we'll start the paperwork which will get you out of here.'

They waited in silence.

★★★★

Five minutes later there was a knock on the interview room door. A policeman put his head round the door.

'Detective Inspector Martin,' he said, 'the Chief Super's here. Says he'd like a word.'

DI Martin picked up his radio and left the interview room. The Chief Superintendent was waiting outside in full uniform.

His first words were, 'Don't tell me you've made any sort of deal.'

DI Martin said nothing.

'If you've made any kind of deal,' the senior officer said firmly, 'that'll be the end of your career.'

The Chief pointed at the interview room door.

'You can't make any sort of deal. Can't you see what'll happen? Every criminal like Dobson will expect a deal. They'll kidnap someone before they do a job. Then if they're caught, they'll want to cut a deal. We just can't do that.'

Before he could say any more DC Green's voice rang out over the radio.

'We've got the girl. I repeat we've got the girl. She's very weak and very scared. But she's alive. Do you hear me? Do you hear me? Over.'

DI Martin looked at his boss and shrugged. Turning round he went back into the interview room.

The DI sat at the table saying nothing. Dobson looked at the inspector expectantly.

DI Martin spoke into his radio.

'Can you repeat the last message? Can you repeat? Over.'

The DI put the radio on the table. DC Green's voice came clearly over the radio.

'We've got the girl. She's very weak, very scared. But she's okay.'

Dobson looked at DI Martin and sneered.

Lifting up his arms from the table he said, 'Okay, now get these cuffs off me.'

The DI looked at him and asked, 'Why?'

'We had a deal,' said Dobson. 'You've got the girl so I go free.'

'What deal?' asked DI Martin.

Dobson turned and looked up at the CCTV camera before snarling.

'You can't back out now. It's all been recorded. Remember? I know my rights.'

DI Martin put his hand in his pocket and dropped a CD onto the table.

He pointed to the CCTV camera.

'See the red light on the CCTV camera? It's flashing,' he said quietly. 'When it's flashing it means there's no CD in the recorder.'

Smiling he added, 'The camera is only recording everything when the light is green.'

Will she die?

DI Martin leaned forward and locked eyes with Dobson.

'There never was a deal,' he hissed.

****